Merry Holidays! 12/99

PIERRE'S DREAM

Thomas   Austin

Jennifer (Hannah) Armstrong

PICTURES BY Susan Gaber

Dial Books for Young Readers

New York

Published by Dial Books for Young Readers
A division of Penguin Putnam Inc.
345 Hudson Street
New York, New York 10014

Designed by Julie Rauer
Printed in Hong Kong on acid-free paper
First Edition
1 3 5 7 9 10 8 6 4 2

Library of Congress Cataloging in Publication Data
Armstrong, Jennifer, date.
Pierre's dream/Jennifer Armstrong; pictures by Susan Gaber.—1st ed.
p. cm.
Summary: Thinking he is dreaming, Pierre, a lazy, foolish man,
shows no fear as he performs many amazing and dangerous circus acts.
ISBN 0-8037-1700-8
[1. Circus—Fiction. 2. Dreams—Fiction.] I. Gaber, Susan, ill. II. Title.
PZ7.A73367Pi 1999 [E]—dc21 98-36179 CIP AC

The illustrations were created with acrylics.

To those of us who are sometimes lazy, foolish,
and prone to naps—as a reminder that we must try walking
the tightrope from time to time.

J.A. and S.G.

Some time ago, in the town of Apt, which is not far from Avignon, there lived a lazy, foolish man named Pierre. He had no job, no interests, and no hobby besides sitting under the olive trees in the afternoon, thinking of dinner.

One day Pierre walked aimlessly through a field, nibbling sunflower seeds and spitting out the husks. In this field was a large tree, and Pierre sat under it to rest. In no time at all he fell asleep and snored loudly enough to startle the crows.

While he slept, the Grand Circus des Étoiles pitched its tents in
the field, ranged its painted wagons around, and strung up a rope
corral for the trick ponies. When Pierre awoke, it was to find himself
in the midst of a bustling village that had not been there before.

"Aha," he said. "I must be dreaming."

He rose and looked about him. He had a wonderful sense of accomplishment. All this, all he surveyed—all was his dream. Pierre was very pleased with himself.

As he stood admiring the work of his imagination, a shout of alarm filled the air.

"The lion! He has escaped!"

Dozens of circus folk fled past Pierre, their colored costumes twinkling in the sunshine.

Then bounding around the corner came a dreadful, snarling lion. His teeth gleamed. His roars made the leaves tremble on the trees. Pierre felt a bit nervous.

"Very realistic," he murmured.

But as it was his dream, or so he thought, he had no fear. "For, of course, I can wake up at any time," he reminded himself.

And so, smiling confidently, Pierre held up one hand.

"Stop, lion!" he commanded. "Back! Go back!"

So strong was Pierre's voice that the lion stopped his charge. He peered around, and then with his tail tucked between his legs the lion turned and slunk back to his cage.

    "Well, that's that," Pierre said. "I'm enjoying this dream very much."

    "Oh, monsieur! You are so brave!" called out the dainty trapeze artist from high above.

    Pierre smiled modestly. "May I join you, mademoiselle?"

    "Please do," she replied, twirling her parasol.

    Pierre examined the pole to which the high wire was strung. He would never attempt such a thing normally, but as it was his dream, or so he thought, Pierre knew he could climb with no effort at all.

Up he went, hand over hand into the air. At the top he had a magnificent view of the countryside all around.

"Yoo-hoo!" called the dainty trapeze artist from the far end of the wire.

Pierre bowed like a courtier, and stepped boldly onto the high wire. It swayed and dipped under his foot.

"Very realistic," he murmured.

But as it was his dream, or so he thought, he had no fear. Pierre walked without hesitation to the middle of the wire.

A crowd of circus folk stared up from below.

"I'll give them a thrill," Pierre said to himself.

"Ooooh!" the crowd gasped as he stood on one foot.

"Aaaah!" the crowd sighed as he hopped up and clicked his heels together.

"Ooooh!" the crowd moaned as Pierre stood on his hands.

With that Pierre skipped cheerfully to the end of the wire and kissed the trapeze artist's hand. He was enjoying this dream very much.

"Can you also swallow swords?" asked the snake charmer.

"Can you also juggle fire?" asked the bearded lady.

"Can you also lie down beneath the elephant's foot?" asked the son of the red-haired clown.

Pierre answered all these questions with a smile and a nod. "But, of course," he replied. In dreams, he knew, one can do anything.

The circus folk voted to make him their ringmaster, as the owner of the Grand Circus des Étoiles was in bed with a stomachache. Pierre put on the top hat and tailcoat, and stretched out his legs for two small boys to polish the tall black boots.

"It's Pierre!" gasped the crowd when he stepped into the ring.

"Pierre!"

"Pierre!"

Pierre bowed to the audience. They knew him, of course, for why should not the people of Apt also be in his dream?

"They all think I am a lazy, foolish man," Pierre told himself. "Tonight they shall see they are wrong."

Pierre cracked his whip. "Send in the ponies!"

One, two, three, four, five—six pretty ponies cantered into the ring, tossing their manes and setting the bells on their headdresses ajingle. Pierre stood in the center, cracking his whip and keeping the ponies at a spirited pace.

"What will he do?" the audience wondered aloud.

"What is Pierre up to?"

The dust flew from under the ponies' hooves and tickled

Pierre's nose. The wind from their passing fanned his cheeks.

"Very realistic," he murmured.

Then with a victorious cry he leaped onto the back of the nearest pony, and stood up with his arms crossed. The audience cheered.

"Pierre!"

"What a marvel!"

"Superb!"

After riding each trick pony in turn, Pierre sent them galloping out of the ring and ordered in the knife thrower. Then, to the astonishment of the audience, he calmly allowed the one-eyed man to throw seventeen daggers around him.

After this he hung by one foot from the trapeze, while juggling flaming hoops above a cage of tigers and panthers from the East. The beasts roared horribly, and the flames singed Pierre's eyebrows. But as it was his dream, or so he thought, he had no fear.

He went on to perform many other daring and death-defying feats, and the audience greeted each new act with wild applause.

"Pierre!"

"What skill and courage!"

"Extraordinary!"

By the end of the evening Pierre had put on nearly the entire circus single-handedly. After the last spectator left the tent, the circus folk lined up and clapped for Pierre as he trod wearily across the sawdust.

"You must rest," whispered the dainty trapeze artist.

Pierre nodded. He was tired. Never before had a dream lasted so long, nor left him so fatigued.

The sickly ringleader rode in on a goat-cart. "The Grand Circus des Étoiles thanks you," he muttered to Pierre.

"It was my pleasure," Pierre replied.

With that he went out and gazed up at the stars in the sky. A long dream, and a very full one, he decided. Then he sat down under a tree, and closed his eyes.

When at last he opened them again, the sun was high in the sky, and the field around him was empty.

"What a dream!" Pierre exclaimed, stretching his arms.

He smiled, and gazed around him contentedly. There was nothing special he wanted to do. There never was. He was truly a lazy, foolish man, with no job, no interests, and no hobby besides sitting under the olive trees in the afternoon, thinking of dinner.

    With a yawn Pierre leaned back against the tree, and knocked the black top hat over his eyes.

    "What's this?" he asked in astonishment.

    He looked wildly around, bewildered and bemused. Next to the tree, on the ground, was a dainty parasol with a slip of paper pinned to the frill.

Pierre picked it up with a trembling hand.

"Au revoir, Pierre," it read.

Slowly, slowly Pierre began to smile. Then he began to laugh. And as he looked up through the leaves of the olive tree, he had much more to think of than just his dinner.